Sticks and Stones

by

Catherine MacPhail

First published in 2005 in Great Britain by
Barrington Stoke Ltd
www.barringtonstoke.co.uk

Reprinted 2006

ISBN 1-842992-95-3
13 digit ISBN 978-1-84299-295-1

Printed in Great Britain by Bell & Bain Ltd

A Note from the Author

Sticks and stones will break my bones, but names will never hurt me.

Rubbish, of course. Names can hurt you. (Though not as much as being hit by a big stick!) Yet we all laugh at clever nicknames, forgetting just how cruel they can sometimes be. I really did know a boy called "Candlegrease", because his nose was always running. Now I can't remember his real name, and that's the cruellest thing of all, I think.

And thinking about all this, Greg began to grow in my mind, the boy who can come up with great nicknames and believes that everyone thinks they're as funny as he does. He doesn't think for a minute that he's hurting anyone, until someone decides to get their own back.

For John Mitchell

Contents

Chapter 1

Sticks and Stones

"Hey, look at those legs!" I let out a low whistle as the girl I called Scooby walked by. She had a face like Scooby Doo himself and that's why I'd picked that nickname for her. But she did have a lovely pair of legs.

Scooby looked at me and scowled. "I hate you, Greg Baxter," she shouted. "I'll get my own back on you one of these days." And she stormed away. Her pals moved off with her. They fluttered round her like a bunch of mad moths. Now, why should Scooby be angry at me? I was trying to say something nice about her. I turned to my friends. "You know, nature gave Scooby a face like a spaniel," I said, "but as soon as you see her legs, you forget about her face. Do you know what I always say?" I went on, "You can say something good about everybody, no matter how ugly they are."

Take my pal, Pinocchio, for example. Now, he's got a nose you could trip over. Even he would have to admit you could use his nose as a ski slope, but he is the best football player in the school. That's something I have always liked about me. I don't mean to sound bigheaded, but it's true. I can always see a good side to everybody.

"You've got nothing good about you anyway, Greg Baxter." I didn't have to turn round to see who said that. It could only be one person. Lucy Kane. She's always on at me. She's as nippy as a sour plum. The Red Menace I call her, because she has so much bright fiery red hair.

"What's your problem?" I asked her.

"I've not got a problem. You're the one with the problem, Greg Baxter. You spend all your time insulting the girls, or making fun of the boys."

Now, that's just not true. "I never badmouth girls," I said loudly. "I like girls!"

"Do you think girls like your comments? I don't think so."

I looked round at my friends. "That's because we don't whistle at her, boys," I said with a laugh.

To tell the truth, I wouldn't dare whistle at Lucy Kane ... she'd probably thump me.

Lucy was always on at me. She was either cross because I was eyeing up the girls, or because I was calling people names. Let's face it, coming up with nicknames is a talent. I'm good at it. What can I say? I am a class act when it comes to nicknames.

Take the guy I call Bumface, for one. He really does have a face like somebody's backside, and red too, like it's been slapped a few times.

I have to admit that Bumface wasn't too happy when he heard what his nickname was. Not that anybody would call him that to his face. He would have thumped them if they had. I had to go into hiding for a few days when he found out. I waited till he calmed down. No-one messes with Bumface. He doesn't like jokes and he's scary. The trouble with Bumface is he has no sense of humour. Not him, or his mate.

I call Bumface's mate Ugg. That's because he looks like a caveman. He should be dragging a club and wearing an animal skin.

Honestly, when you see Bumface and Ugg together they give horror movies a bad name.

But do they ever laugh at themselves? No.

4

That was the problem with Lucy Kane as well. She had no sense of humour. Now she stood in front of me with a face as hard as stone. One smile would crack it and she would crumble like dust. I wish.

"Get on your bike," I said.

"Thank you," she snapped back.

Just then the school loudspeakers crackled into life. We all stopped to listen. The headmaster was about to make an announcement.

"I bet he's going to tell us that I've just been picked as Brad Pitt's double in a new movie," I said with a grin.

"Sssh!" Lucy tutted at me.

"I have some very bad news, I'm afraid." The headmaster's grim voice echoed round the school. "One of our pupils, Tony Harris, was mugged as he was walking through the school car park last night. His mobile phone was stolen. I had no choice but to call the police and they will be here shortly." Then, all at once, his voice roared out so loud I thought he was about to have a heart attack. "When I find out who did this they'll be very sorry!"

I looked around at Pinocchio. "Who's Tony Harris?" I was trying to remember who he was. It came to me in a flash. "Oh, Fat Tony … the Incredible Bulk."

Lucy gave me a push and I almost went flying down the stairs.

"There you go again!" she yelled at me. "His name's Tony Harris. And this is nothing to laugh about. He's been mugged and someone's stolen his mobile phone."

"Goodness – how's he going to phone for all his take-away pizzas now?" I asked with a laugh.

That was funny. My friends laughed too. Only Lucy didn't seem to think it was funny.

I hate women who don't have a sense of humour.

But I didn't laugh later on, when the police came. They roared up in a police car and two of them marched into the school and went straight to the headmaster's office. There was a young police constable who all the girls fancied, and an officer who looked like a big slug.

The whole school was talking about how Fat Tony had been mugged. Everyone was asking if he'd seen who'd mugged him. Some people said he had. The police thought they knew who it was. Someone from our school.

I was standing by my locker. I noticed it was open a crack. That was funny! I must have forgotten to lock it. The school loudspeakers crackled again. The headmaster announced that the police officer wanted to speak to us.

"We've come to the school today to try out a little ex-per-i-ment," the Slug spoke very slowly. "An experiment which we hope will root out the thief."

Me and my friends all looked at each other. We didn't understand what was going on.

I looked over and saw Bumface scowling ... no, wait a minute, that was him smiling. And Ugg was staring up at the loudspeakers too. He looked just like Fred Flintstone on a bad day.

"I wonder what kind of experiment he means," Pinocchio said to me.

The Slug was still speaking. "The victim had his mobile phone stolen," he said. "And, as some of you know, this mobile had a very special ringtone."

Who could forget that? Tony had paid a lot of money to get that ringtone. No mobile in the school sounded like Fat Tony's.

"So," the Slug went on, "we're going to phone Tony's mobile. Who knows, our experiment might work. We might be lucky. We might hear the missing mobile and find out where it is. And that will give us a clue about who stole it."

I turned to Pinocchio. "As if anybody's daft enough to keep the stolen mobile in school ... you'd have to be brain dead to do that."

All at once, the air was filled with the sound of Tony's mobile ringing. The ringing was coming from a locker close by. So someone *had* been that stupid. The mobile *was* in school.

But who had it?

At that moment the Slug came out of the headmaster's office. He was staring right at me. I couldn't think why. He strode up the corridor, walking towards the sound. He kept on looking right at me. I moved out of the way to let him pass by. But he didn't walk past me. He came to a halt right beside me.

I didn't know what to do next. "But ... eh, but ..." I stammered.

The Slug opened the door of my locker.

And Tony's phone was there.

Chapter 2
It wasn't me!

"It wasn't me!" I had been saying I was innocent ever since the police officer had dragged me into the headmaster's room. And I do mean *dragged*. It was really embarrassing. The Slug had got me by the collar and almost lifted me off my feet. Now that can't be right. That *must* be against my human rights or something.

"We found the mobile in your locker," the Slug told me again.

"It was a plant!" I said.

11

"No, it was a phone." He chuckled as if he had said something really funny. He thought he was a comedian. I hate funny cops.

"Well, *I* didn't put it there."

"If it wasn't you ... who was it?"

My brain was in overdrive. I was trying to stay cool and calm, the way heroes always are in films. But to be frank I was in a cold sweat. All I could think about was that my mum was going to kill me when she found out about all of this.

"Tony Harris couldn't see who grabbed him, but he thinks it might have been you. Now we've found the mobile in *your* locker, I think we've got the proof we need."

I was shocked. "How could Tony have said it was me?" I shouted. "What a big liar!" That's when, all at once, I knew who'd put the mobile in my locker. "Fat Tony put the mobile there," I said. "It was the Incredible Bulk himself who did it. I bet it was him."

The Slug leaned closer to me. I could feel his hot breath on my face. "And why would young Tony put his own phone into your locker and give himself a black eye?"

"To get his own back," I told him.

"To get his own back," he said. "What for? What have you done to Tony?"

I shut up at that point. I was remembering Fat Tony yelling at me, just a few days before. "I'll get you for this, Baxter," he'd shouted. Just because one day, after dinner time, I'd put the leftovers from a few plates – well, maybe more than a few – into his locker with a note –

I know you'll eat anything!

It was just a bit of fun. Everybody else had a laugh. Tony just didn't see the funny side.

I knew the Slug could see guilt all over my face. Big time.

G-U-I-L-T.

I didn't answer his question for a long time. Then, at last, I said, "I've never done anything to Tony."

I don't think the Slug believed me.

I was allowed to go back to my class. Ha! As if I could learn anything after that. I soon found out how fast a whole school, and your so-called friends, can turn against you.

By now everyone in the school knew that Tony had told the police it was me who had mugged him.

"You're a rat," someone said. "How could you mug Tony just to get your hands on his mobile?"

"It wasn't me!"

14

"How sick can you get – following Tony out of school and giving him a black eye!" someone else said.

"It wasn't me!"

Even Pinocchio, my best pal, thought I was guilty. That was what hurt the most. "You told me the other day it would be a laugh to take his mobile, to stop him phoning for food," he reminded me. "You said you'd be doing him a favour."

He was right. I had said that. In front of everyone. And now they were all glaring at me. I looked around at my friends.

"It was only a joke," I told them. "Honest. It wasn't me that mugged Tony."

That was all I seemed to say for the rest of the day. "It wasn't me!"

Not that anybody believed me. It was even worse at lunch break. Nobody would sit beside me in the school canteen. I carried my tray up to the table I always sat at but all my friends spread themselves out so there was no room for me. I ended up sitting in a corner, eating on my own.

It wasn't fair. I hadn't done anything wrong. I couldn't understand how Tony's mobile got into my locker. I just knew that I hadn't put it there.

The Slug was waiting for me at the gates when school finished. He was coming home with me so he could tell my mum and dad about what had happened.

I was very scared about what they'd say. It was even worse than I'd expected. They went mad. My mum's a drama queen at the best of times. She burst into tears. "A son of mine, arrested. In jail. A criminal." She sat down on the settee and cried.

The Slug tried to calm her down. "It hasn't come to that yet, madam," he told her.

But my mum didn't believe him. I think she'd been watching too many prison movies.

My dad went mental. "This is one of your practical jokes that just went too far!" Even my parents seemed to believe I'd done this terrible thing – mugged Tony and nicked his mobile. And, of course, it didn't help that Tony had accused me. "It wasn't me!" I kept yelling at them.

"Have you got an alibi for last night, son?" the Slug asked me. "Someone who can say for sure that you couldn't have mugged Tony because you were somewhere else?"

Before I could answer my dad spoke for me. "No. He hasn't. He came home late from school last night. He told us he'd been going to meet someone. He didn't say who it was."

And that was when I remembered the text message I'd had from Jamila Jones yesterday afternoon. She wanted me to meet her in the school car park. I've fancied Jamila for a long time. And I've always thought she had a soft spot for me.

I'd gone to meet up with her and I'd waited for an hour. But she hadn't turned up. How could I tell that to the Slug, or to anyone else for that matter? Tell the world I got stood up? Come on.

But if I couldn't tell, it meant I didn't have an alibi.

"So, let's get this straight," the Slug went on slowly. "Tony says it was you. His mobile was found in your locker. And you don't have an alibi."

All I could answer was, "It wasn't me," but I didn't sound so sure of myself now. I was beginning to think my memory was playing tricks on me. Could I have forgotten that I'd mugged him? Goodness, even I was beginning to think I was guilty.

I was waiting for the Slug to put handcuffs on me and drag me off to prison. It didn't happen of course. He didn't even take me down to the police station. But that night was the worst of my life.

I didn't want to go to school next day but my mum made me. You know what mums are like. "Face up to things, Greg," she said.

So I faced up to it. Hardly anyone even looked at me as I walked through the school gates. Nobody said hello. I dragged my feet along the corridor and opened my locker. Inside was a stuffed rat. Its head had been torn off.

"Who did this?" My voice seemed to echo through the whole school.

Nobody answered. Nobody even looked my way. "I don't know who mugged Fat Tony ... But it wasn't me!!!!!" I yelled so loud I thought the windows were going to crack. "It wasn't me," I said again, softly this time.

"I don't think it was you either."

I turned round fast to see who'd said that. At last someone believed me!

When I saw who it was you could have knocked me down with a gust of bad breath.

It was Lucy Kane.

Chapter 3

Enter Lucy

Lucy! The Red Menace. Was she the only one in the school who believed I was innocent? Could she be having me on? Had to be.

"Did I hear you right?" I wanted to know. She took a step closer. I took a step back. I was sure she was about to attack me.

"Of course you're innocent," she said. "You don't have the brains to be a criminal mastermind. A criminal idiot, maybe."

For a minute, I wasn't sure that I wanted her on my side. Not if she was going to insult me like that.

"But they found Fat Tony's mobile in my locker," I said. "How do you explain that?"

"That's simple. Even *you* could figure that out. If you didn't put it there, stupid, somebody else did. Somebody who wants you to get the blame."

It took me a few seconds to work that out. "You mean … I've been framed?"

"It would seem like that, yeah."

"But who would want to frame me?" As soon as I said that Lucy began to laugh. As if I had said something funny.

"Let's see," she said, tapping her teeth with her nail. "Can you think of anyone who doesn't like you in this school?"

Then, before I could answer "no", she began to laugh again. She laughed so much I thought she was going to choke. I wish.

"Or should I say ... can you think of anyone who *likes* you in this school?"

Now that really hurt. "What do you mean by that? Everybody likes me. I'm a very popular boy."

She laughed even more. "Who told you that?"

I was about to tell her, but she never lets you get a word in.

"You make up cruel nicknames for people, you play nasty tricks on them," she went on quickly. "And you think people like you? You even insult your best pal."

"Pinocchio likes his nickname."

"Does he? So, where is he now, your best pal?"

She was right. My best pal wasn't speaking to me. It really hurt that he had turned against me. But I wasn't going to admit that to Lucy.

"The nicknames I make up aren't cruel. They're funny."

"Funny to you, maybe. Do you think Tony likes being called the Incredible Bulk?"

"There you are, then – it's him, isn't it? I said so from the beginning. It was Fat Tony who told the police I'd mugged him and he planted the mobile in my locker. He said he was going to get me. Just because he can't take a joke." I was ready to leg it out of school and go to his house to get him. "I'm going to kill him. He's about to lose two stone in two minutes when I rip his head off."

Lucy grabbed me back. "Think about what you just said, brain box. Tony hasn't been back at school since the evening he was mugged. How could he have put the mobile in

24

your locker? And, did he give himself a black eye? I don't think so."

Then it was like a light was switched on in my head. I worked out what was going on. "He's in it with somebody else," I said.

Even as I said that, I was thinking that Tony must have let someone hit him, punch him so hard he had a black eye. Had he done that just to get back at me? Did he hate me that much? Did anybody?

Lucy was looking hard at me. "So, why didn't you have an alibi for that night? Where were you?"

That was a question I didn't want her to ask. I didn't want anybody to know Jamila had stood me up. And I *really* didn't want Lucy Kane to know that. "None of your business," I said.

"Yes it is! I'm trying to help you. Come on, tell me."

"I got a date mixed up. I went to meet somebody and it was the wrong day, that's all."

Lucy was shaking her head. Her red hair swung about and almost hit me in the face. "You're lying, Greg Baxter. Come on ... how can I help you if you don't tell me the truth?"

"I was meant to be going out with a girl," I admitted at last.

Lucy began to laugh again. "And you got stood up."

"I did not."

"Yes, you did. Who stood you up?"

I knew as soon as I told her she would laugh again. "Jamila Jones, and if you laugh at me I'll thump you."

She laughed at me. Of course I didn't thump her. I never hit girls. In fact, I never hit anyone. That's what I mean about me being a really nice guy.

"Why shouldn't Jamila Jones want to go out with me? She's the best-looking bird in the school."

"Maybe because you're always calling her a 'bird' for a start."

"Anyway, it was just a mix-up."

Now I was trying to think if I'd ever done anything to upset Jamila. "Do you think maybe Jamila is in this with Tony? Maybe she punched him to make it look real."

Lucy sniggered. "Jamila? Punch anybody? She'd be too scared she'd break a nail."

That made me think that Lucy didn't like Jamila much. Was it because Jamila was so good-looking? Could be. But when I looked at Lucy, she was pretty fit herself. That hair of hers was something else. A mass of rich red curls. Not my type, of course. As soon as she opened her mouth she wasn't my type.

"So when did you ask her out?"

"I didn't. She asked me."

She laughed so loud at that, everyone looked over at us. "Jamila asked you out?" she said. "In your dreams."

"She did! Well, in fact she sent me a text. I'll show you the message. I kept it."

Right away I was sorry I'd told her that.

"Oh, that's *so sweet*. You kept it." She grabbed the mobile from me. "Let me see."

Meet me in car park. 4pm. I fancy u. jamila.

"You really do think you're something, don't you? Thinking she'd fancy you. She never even looks at you."

"She's playing hard to get."

"This text could have come from anyone. Do you know the mobile number it came from?"

I gave a shrug. "It must be Jamila's mobile number, I suppose."

Lucy pressed the buttons on my mobile and got back to where the sender's number was printed. "No," she said, shaking her head, "this is not Jamila's number. But I know whose number it is." She waited a while before she went on. "This text came from Tony's phone. It's his mobile number. I think he wanted to get back at you for all the names you've called him."

"I'll kill him!" I said, ready to run off again.

Just then the bell rang for class to start. "We'd better go," Lucy said. "I'll meet you at lunchtime. And please, no murder until we find out the truth about all this."

I walked slowly into my class. I didn't feel
alone anymore. Now I had the Red Menace on
my side, even if all she did was insult me.
I looked around at everyone in my class.
They were all ignoring me and I felt bad
knowing that one of them hated me so much.

Chapter 4

A Warning

I couldn't listen to a word Bushy, our teacher, was saying. His beard looked even more like a bush that morning. I kept looking around at my class and thinking about who was behind this plan to get me.

Who hated me so much?

It couldn't possibly be Pinocchio. We'd been pals for too long. He may have been against me now, but that was only because he thought I'd mugged Tony.

Was it Willie the Wimp? He was a skinny boy who jumped every time you said boo to him. I know he was angry because I'd locked him in the science cupboard where Bushy had his collection of snakes. They weren't live snakes! I mean, they were in jars. They couldn't hurt Willie. But still he yelled and he screamed and he'd told everyone he would get me for it.

Could it be Candlegrease? I picked that nickname for him because his nose was always running. Was he still upset because I'd sneaked into the headmaster's office one day and I'd announced over the loudspeakers that while Candlegrease had a cold he'd hand out free green candles to everyone, made from all his snot.

What *was* his real name ...?

Trying to work it out made me realise I couldn't remember the real names of most of my mates. All I ever used were their nicknames. Did that bother them so much?

Then I thought of something else. Did I have a nickname, too?

No. Of course I didn't. I mean, what nickname could anybody call me? I had good teeth, a headful of brown hair and a great personality.

All round nice guy. That's me. And I would thump anybody who didn't agree with that.

But then I started to think about how many of my mates at some time or other had said, "I'll get you for this."

Was everyone in this together?

Were they all trying to teach me a lesson?

Just as we were coming out of the classroom, the headmaster asked me to come to his office. "Young Tony is returning to school tomorrow," he said. "I'm warning you now, you're not to go anywhere near him."

"Wait a minute, sir. Have I got the right to ask why he's got it in for me?"

The headmaster looked grim. I could see a nerve in his cheek throbbing like a time bomb. "Are you still insisting that you're innocent?"

"It's the truth, sir. I'm an innocent man!"

The headmaster didn't look as if he believed me. "I'm telling you now, boy, if Tony even whispers that you're bothering him you'll be in deep trouble."

I didn't like to remind him that I was in deep trouble already.

At lunchtime I felt like going home, I was so fed up. But it would have been every bit as bad, if not worse, at home. So I stayed at school. Even though half the school glared at me as if I was some kind of mad monster and the other half just ignored me.

The only person who made the day bearable was the Red Menace, Lucy.

When she walked into the canteen, her eyes swept all round the tables looking for me. I was in a corner on my own. I jumped up and waved at her like a shipwrecked sailor who has just seen a ship coming to rescue him at last.

I was so happy that one person, at least, was still talking to me.

Everyone watched as she came up to me. "They'll stop talking to *you* next," I told her as she sat down beside me.

Lucy gave a shrug. "I don't care. I don't do what everyone else does. I do what I want. Even if that means sitting and having my lunch with an idiot like you."

See what I mean? Lucy always gives you a compliment and then whams you with an insult straight after.

She bit into her burger. "I've had a chat with Jamila," she said, spitting crumbs all over the table. "She didn't send you any text ... which didn't surprise me at all."

"So, she didn't ask me out on a date?" I said, and I tried not to sound too let down.

Lucy was grinning from ear to ear. "I'll not tell you just what she did say when I asked her, but it was something like 'Me? Go out with that ugly git? Is he mad?'"

"She's playing hard to get," I said again. I didn't want Lucy to see I felt upset. How would *you* feel if the girl of your dreams said that about you? "She could be lying," I went on. "I don't trust beautiful women."

"You trust me, I hope," Lucy said.

"I said I don't trust *beautiful* women ... of course I trust you."

In fact, I have to admit Lucy *is* really pretty. As she'd walked across the canteen towards me I couldn't help looking at her legs. She's got great legs. But I wanted to say something to hurt her after what she'd told me about Jamila. She got so angry, she nearly pushed what was left of her burger in my face.

"No wonder somebody's out to get you, ratface! You say some really mean things."

Things could have got nasty at that point, but just then Lucy's mobile began to buzz. She had a text message.

She was still glaring at me as she began to read it. Then the look on her face changed and she handed me her phone. "Read that," she said.

I took the phone from her.

Hes gettin wots cumin 2 him, said the text.
U will 2 if u help him.

Chapter 5

Getting my own back

I gulped and looked round the canteen. There were quite a few people who had their mobiles out. Some were busy texting. One of them had to be the person who'd just sent the text to Lucy. It had to be someone who could see us together, someone in the school canteen.

Then I saw that Pinocchio was looking over at me. He had his mobile in his hand. He turned away from me and slipped it in his pocket. I felt my spine turn to ice. I'd thought it was someone in this canteen. But not Pinocchio. Not my best friend.

"It says 'unknown number'," Lucy said as she looked up from her mobile. "But it has to be someone here, someone who's watching us and sitting at one of these tables." Lucy didn't seem too worried about the threat. "We know something else too."

"We do?" I hadn't a clue what we knew.

"Of course we do," Lucy looked hard at me as I tried and tried to think of something clever to say, or to work out what the clue to solving the whole mystery was. I wanted to be like Sherlock Holmes. I knew the person who'd sent the text must be someone with a mobile. But, after that I had no more ideas.

"I'm going to die of old age before you work it out," Lucy said. She didn't sound one bit like Doctor Watson, who was Sherlock Holmes' trusty sidekick. "Think about it, moron, someone has just sent me a text," she went on.

Then I worked it out. "It must be someone who knows your mobile number," I said, dead chuffed with myself.

"And I don't give out my number to anybody."

"I don't even know your number," I said.

"You're the last person I would give it to."

There she went again with more insults. I waited a while and then I asked, "So, who does know your number?"

"Some of the girls," Lucy said, "The ones you're always whistling at. Some of the boys know my number too. But you're always playing tricks on them. There are a lot of people who'd like to get back at you."

I had to ask. "Does Pinocchio know your number?"

She nodded and I felt grim. "How?" I asked.

"Our mums are best friends." She stared at me. "Come on," she said, "do you think Pinocchio's really in on this with Tony?"

And I didn't. Not really. But I felt sick when I remembered the look on his face when he dropped his mobile into his pocket.

"It might be better for you if you stopped helping me," I said. "You might end up with a black eye as well."

She didn't say a word for a moment, and my heart sank. Instead of feeling my heart beating in my chest, I started feeling it thumping somewhere deep inside my stomach. I didn't want Lucy to do what the text said.

I should have remembered. Lucy never does what anyone tells her. "You've got to be joking," she said. "This is just getting interesting."

School felt weird the next day when Tony came back. I couldn't have got near him even if I'd wanted to. Everywhere he went, a group of friends went round with him to protect him. Ha! Before he was attacked he didn't have that many friends. Maybe the person who'd mugged him had done him a favour.

My problem was I wanted everyone to know that "person" wasn't me.

Every time Tony passed anywhere near me, he looked over at me quickly. Maybe he thought I might pounce on him. To tell the truth that's what I felt like doing. I wanted to jump on him and make him tell me the truth. He'd stuck me right in it. I was right to be mad at him.

I got my chance after lunch break. I bumped into Tony in, of all places, the boys' toilets. That was the only place his minders let him go on his own. Let's face it, it would take a real, true friend to go into the bog with you. He walked into the toilets just as I was coming out of one of the cubicles.

As soon as he saw me, he did an about-turn to go back out of the door. I was having none of that. Fate had thrown us together. I wasn't going to waste the chance to ask him what was going on.

"Hold it, you!" I hissed. I didn't shout, in case his minders were right outside the door. "What's going on, Tony? You know it wasn't me who mugged you."

"It *was* you. They found my mobile in your locker."

"Someone put it there. You're in this with someone else. Who is it?" Tony's face went pale. I could see I was right. "Who is it?"

Instead of telling me, Tony tried to make a run for it, but in Fat Tony's case it was more like a roll. I grabbed him back. "Someone put your mobile in my locker, Tony, and you know who. I'm going to make you tell the truth." I began to shake him. He let out a yell as if I was cutting his throat. I wasn't even hurting him. I was only giving him a gentle little shake. But that one yell alerted his minders and they came crashing into the bog.

Bumface and Ugg came in first, would you believe? Now that's never happened before! They never help anybody. Pinocchio was there too. He pulled Tony away from me and glared at me. "Someone needs to teach you a lesson!" he said.

I'm sure he would have thumped me then and there if the headmaster hadn't arrived at that minute and rescued me. Rescued me! That's a joke! The headmaster pushed his way into the toilets and he roared at me. Then he sent me home in disgrace.

At home, it was even worse than yesterday. My gran was there too this time. "You're going to send me to an early grave, boy," she wailed.

Early grave? She's 91. I think she's missed the early grave by quite a few years.

Mum did a bit more of her drama queen act. "What are you doing to me, Greg? How am I ever going to face the Ladies Keep Fit Class again?"

Then Dad went on and on at me for an hour. All in all, it was a bad day. Until, that is, Lucy phoned.

"I've had a chat with Tony," she said. "He's scared of someone."

"Me?" I asked. I remembered the way he'd kept looking over at me all that morning.

"No, not you. You're a weed. Why would anyone be scared of you?" Lucy always manages to make me feel worse, somehow. She whispered down the phone in a voice so soft, I could hardly hear her. "I don't know who he's scared of. All he said was, 'I'll get another black eye if anyone sees me talking to you'."

Chapter 6
Teamwork

Lucy came over to my house later that night. It was the first time a girl had ever visited me at home.

"I didn't know you had a girlfriend," my dad said.

"She is not my girlfriend." I mean, Lucy, my girlfriend? Get real.

"I think it's very good of her to stick by you when no-one else has." This was my mum talking.

"She's not my girlfriend," I told her.

But do they ever listen?

"You don't deserve her," my gran said.

By the time Lucy arrived my mum thought she was wonderful, my gran had baked her a cake, and my dad was almost making up a speech for our wedding.

Lucy only laughed her head off when I told her.

I wish she *could* laugh her head off. I'd love to see it rolling down the street. Maybe then I wouldn't have to listen to her going on at me any more.

"They don't think I'm that hard up, do they? I don't need *you* as a boyfriend!" she giggled.

"What do you mean? There's plenty of girls who would love to have a date with me."

"Name one," she said.

I didn't even bother to answer her. But I decided then and there that after all this was over I would never speak to her again.

I mean, a guy can only take so much.

"So what about Tony?" I asked her.

I knew she was dying to tell me all she'd found out. She's such a show-off. "I think the only reason someone gave Tony the black eye and stole his mobile was to get back at you. And I think Tony knows who it is and is too scared to tell us."

I jumped to my feet. "I'll make him tell me."

Lucy shook her head. "Don't you see? You're part of the reason Tony's not telling the full story. He's scared of the person who's done this to him, but he's not telling who it is because he wants to get back at you. All those names you call him, they're hurtful.

You think you're being funny, but it's not funny for him."

"Some people just can't take a joke," I said.

Lucy thought for a bit, then she said, "The trouble is half the school wants to get back at you."

I'd had plenty of time to think about that. I'd only ever tried to be funny. I never meant any real harm.

It seemed now a lot of people just hadn't seen the funny side.

I thought, too, about who was behind this. And there was one thing I was sure of now. It couldn't be my best friend, Pinocchio. He couldn't scare anybody. He was too nice a guy. The thought made me feel good.

It made me realise something else too. A lot of people might have it in for me, but there's only a few people in our school that Tony's scared of.

As soon as I understood that, I thought of Bumface and Ugg. I told Lucy.

"No wonder Bumface and Ugg were glued to Tony today," I said. "It wasn't to protect him at all. They were making sure he didn't talk to me."

But Lucy wasn't sure. She said we needed proper proof.

"In this country you're innocent until they prove you guilty." She wants to be a lawyer when she grows up – and she talks like one already!

"I'm going to phone Tony now," she said.

Tony's mum answered the phone. I could hear her laughing and talking to Lucy as if she liked her. Lucy chatted for a while. Maybe Tony's mum thought Lucy was Tony's girlfriend. He could have her. Then Tony came to the phone.

I was dying to grab the phone off Lucy and shout down the line at Tony, but Lucy had warned me to keep my mouth shut.

"Tony," she said softly, "I'm going to ask you something and you don't have to answer. Don't say a word. But if you don't answer then I'll know I'm right, OK?"

I could hear Tony mumble something back to her.

"Was it John and Dave who stole your mobile? And then did they make you tell everyone it was Greg who'd done it?"

John and Dave. Who the heck were they? I thought to myself.

Then I remembered – those were Ugg's and Bumface's real names.

Lucy was quiet now. There was a long silence. "OK, Tony," Lucy said at last. "I understand, and I want you to know that I've got a plan. A plan that won't get you into any trouble, and that's going to clear Greg's name."

The long silence ended at that point.

I could hear Tony shouting, "Why should I help that big git? He deserves everything he gets."

Well, I like that. How dare he! After all I was doing for him!

"I totally agree, Tony," Lucy said into the phone. "But I want to help *you*. You don't want to be scared of John forever, do you?"

"I suppose I don't," I heard Tony say. "What's your plan?"

"I'll ring you back in a minute," Lucy replied. She put down the phone.

I looked at her closely. "Yes, smart-arse ... just what is your plan?"

"I haven't a clue," she said.

Chapter 7
Gotcha!

In the end, it was me who came up with the plan, and it was a simple one. "Just like you," Lucy had to say.

I'd seen it work out on lots of detective movies. It would work now. We needed someone to make a confession and say they'd done it. My name would be cleared. And also, if someone owned up, it wouldn't look as if Tony had grassed on anyone.

I was going to hide a tape recorder in my shirt. My mum had a tiny tape recorder that she used for work. It was just the right size to put in my pocket. Then I was going to trick Ugg into telling us everything and it would all be recorded.

I chose Ugg to trick because he's so dim and it would be easy-peasy.

I felt a bit stupid with a tape recorder stuck in the top pocket of my shirt, but the bump looked as if it might be a mobile.

I saw Ugg next day standing by his locker, picking his nose.

"Better watch your brains don't fall out there," I called to him.

He looked fierce, but then he always does. "What d'you want?" he growled.

"I want to talk to you." I pretended I was looking around for somewhere to go. In fact, Lucy had already decided where we should go for our little "talk". The headmaster's office. I thought that was a risky place to choose.

Lucy reminded me that the headmaster's never there on Fridays. He has to go to meetings all Friday afternoon. And no-one ever goes into the headmaster's office when he isn't there. Lucy said it would be the most private place in the school, most of all if we went there when the school secretary was having her break.

"Let's go in here," I said to Ugg and I walked down the corridor to the headmaster's office. I held the door open for Ugg to go in.

Ugg looked puzzled. "What do you want to talk to me about?" he muttered.

I waited until he was inside the office and I closed the door. "Look, U ... em." It was hard to remember his real name. "Dave, isn't it? Look, pal. I know what's been happening with Fat Tony. It was you and B ..." Again, I had a real problem remembering Bumface's real name. "It was you and John ... yes, John," I went on. "It was you two that mugged Tony and took his mobile. One of you put that mobile in my locker. And then I got the blame. Am I right?"

It took Ugg a while to say anything. I could almost hear the wheels of his brain spinning round, trying to work it all out. "Did Tony tell you that?" he said at last.

I wanted to say, "Yes, he did." Tony deserved it. But I knew that Lucy was listening outside.

Lucy had warned me not to say anything about Tony. I shook my head. "Tony hasn't said a thing," I said. "He was too scared to talk to me. But I know what happened. I worked it out. I know it was Bu ... John, that made you do it. If you just tell me the truth, I'll make sure your name's kept out of it."

I didn't think that Ugg would grass on his mate. He's not got the brains for that.

But I thought he might blab out the whole thing by mistake ... and then I would have it all on tape. That's what always happens on TV. The cops trick the baddies into telling them everything.

I don't think Ugg had seen the same TV programmes as me. "I don't know what you're talking about," he said.

"Come on, you and John set me up. Admit it, and good on you! I've been a bit of an idiot at times. You were only getting your own back." I hated saying that bit, but Lucy said I had to. "So, let's forgive and forget, eh?"

Ugg didn't seem to care. "You *are* an idiot, but I don't know what you're on about."

This wasn't working out the way it was meant to. I was ready to shout out to Lucy, "Do something!" but at that moment, someone else did something.

The door flew open and Bumface crashed into the office. He looked from Ugg to me, and back again. His face was red with rage. He looked like a ripe tomato ready to burst open.

"What have you told him?" he yelled at Ugg. "Have you opened your big mouth?"

"Shut up, John," Ugg said, his voice cold as ice.

"Don't tell him anything," Bumface said, and then, all at once, he grabbed me and started shaking me. "What are you up to, pal? Think you're clever, do you?"

My mind was racing. It was all going to work out – and Bumface was going to be the one to confess.

That's when it happened.

Bumface was shaking me so hard, the tape recorder jumped out of my pocket and fell to the floor. It rolled across the carpet.

Bumface looked at me and grinned. "Think you were being clever did you? You've seen too many detective movies, Greg old boy." He lifted his foot and crushed the mini tape recorder under his heel. So much for my plan.

He gripped my neck tight. "That's your trouble, you think you're cleverer than everyone else. But you won't get the better of me! Nobody gets the better of me. I always get my own back.

"Fat Tony stepped out of line and I got my own back on him, didn't I? Gave him a black eye and I took his mobile. Then I told him he'd get another black eye if he didn't say it was you that done it. I knew everybody heard you that day when you said you were going to take Tony's mobile. Clever or what? I've got my own back on two of you at the same time."

Ugg spoke then. "Shut up, John."

But John didn't listen. Now that he'd started nothing was going to stop him. Here he was confessing everything and I didn't have a tape recorder handy.

"You'll not be calling me stupid names again, will you, pal? And just to finish things off, I think I'll give *you* a black eye as well. Call it self-defence. No-one trusts you now anyway." With that, Bumface lifted his fist to thump me.

I was having none of that. I jumped back. I forgot he was still gripping my throat and I almost choked. His fist just missed my face, but it caught me on the chin. It felt as if he'd broken my jaw. So then I lifted my foot and gave him a hard kick on the shins.

He let out a yell and swore. "Give me a hand here, Dave!" he shouted.

Ugg was ready to do just that, when suddenly a mad female seemed to fly out from under the desk, screaming. It was Lucy. Her hair was streaming behind her like fire. She threw herself on top of Ugg and clung on to his back like a rucksack. He tried to shake her off while Bumface thumped me again. And thumped ... and thumped. I had no chance to fight back. He had my throat held so tight I couldn't even yell.

I was on the floor, almost finished, when the door burst open and the headmaster rushed into the office.

"It wasn't our fault, sir!" Bumface said at once. He dropped me. "Lucy and Greg got us in here and then they attacked us." He stood back and tried to look innocent. "It was self-defence, sir."

The headmaster shook his head. "No use lying now, John. I've heard everything. The whole school has. You've just told everyone what's been going on – on the school's loudspeakers."

I looked over at Lucy. She was still clinging onto Ugg. She gave me a wink. Now I knew. Lucy had been in the office all the time. She'd got in there before me and Ugg and she'd been hiding under the desk. That was where the switch for the loudspeakers was. I tried to wink back at her, but instead, I conked out.

Chapter 8
Better than one

So, at last my name was cleared. I'd saved Tony and I'd given Bumface a well-deserved thumping as well. No. That's not true. *He* had given me the thumping. When the school heard our fight on the loudspeakers, everyone cheered each time I yelled in pain. They took bets, too, on who would win. And no-one betted on me.

And of course, it was Lucy who got the credit for finding out what had really happened.

The people who didn't want to know me when they thought I was guilty were slapping me on the back now. It was good to be pals with Pinocchio again. No. I don't call him Pinocchio now. I'm never going to use nicknames again.

My best friend's name is Ben.

Ben came up to me next day and he put out his hand. "Sorry, I wasn't much of a pal. It wasn't too good of me to think you could have done a thing like that," he said. He looked a bit sheepish.

I didn't tell him that, for a time, I thought he was one of the guys who was setting me up. I guess we're even. Me and Ben.

Even the beautiful Jamila was almost friendly. When I walked into the school canteen a few days later she was sitting with her pals and she looked up at me with those big dark eyes of hers, and she smiled. I'd never seen Jamila smiling before. In fact,

she's one moody-looking girl. So the smile
was something of a shock. So were her teeth.
I've never seen so many. She looked like a
hungry shark. It was the scariest thing I've
ever seen in my life.

I went quickly over to the table Lucy was
sharing with the Incredible Bulk.

No. I'll never call him the Incredible Bulk
again. Lucy had a long talk with me ... in fact
it was a lecture. She told me that I deserved
everything that had happened to me. I'd
called people names and played nasty tricks
on them. Lucy said you should never judge
someone just by the way they look. Look at
Ugg, for one. I don't mean Ugg, I mean Dave.
It turns out he isn't as daft as he looks. He
was the clever one between him and Bum ... I
mean John. It's going to be hard to remember
all these new names.

Anyway, poor old Tony was sitting beside
Lucy. He was staring at a plate of lettuce.

Lucy has put him on a diet. She drives you mad. I've never met anyone so annoying. She's lucky no-one's murdered her before now.

"Oh, I thought you'd go and sit with your girlfriend," she said and she glared across at Jamila.

"I think I've gone off her," I said. "She looks just like Jaws."

Lucy snapped at me. "What did you promise about nicknames? No more, OK? Even for Jamila."

"OK, boss," I said. I looked at Tony. He was staring at me as if he needed help.

"Lucy's forcing me to eat this," he said sadly.

I promised I'd slip him a packet of crisps later.

Then I thought, *Why was Lucy glaring at Jamila?*

Why would she be looking like that? I mean, when you glare at somebody it means you don't like them ... or ... you're jealous of them.

Jealous?

That was it.

Lucy was jealous. Jealous because she thought I fancied Jamila.

I'd said to myself that I would never see Lucy again after this was all over. Yet here I was looking for her in the canteen. Why had I done that? Because she'd been the only one who'd stuck by me. She thought I was innocent. When I looked at her closely, I saw she wasn't bad-looking at all. That hair of hers is something else. When she came flying out from under that desk she looked like a warrior queen from the history books. You would never be scared to go out on a dark night with Lucy Kane by your side.

"What are you staring at?" she said.

She's such a lady. "What am I staring at? I was thinking you're not bad-looking. You know you could be pretty fit if you kept your mouth shut long enough."

Her eyes, wow, her bright green eyes flashed at me. "And you might look OK if you put a bag over your head."

See what I mean? It's impossible to have a proper talk with her. "You don't know how lucky you are to have me sitting next to you. There's lots of girls would give their right arm to go out with me."

"Name one," she said.

I took a chance then. "Lucy Kane," I said.

And do you know what she did? She smiled. She gave a big smile and she didn't tell me to stop messing around. This could have been a romantic moment.

Not with Lucy Kane. She hasn't a clue how to be romantic.

"I know, madness must run in my family," she said.

I was just about to stuff a hot pie in her face when another boy came up to us. I always called him Toilet Breath. OK, I promised I would never use nicknames again, so don't tell Lucy I said that, but at that moment I couldn't remember what his name was. His breath smelt awful!

Tony said, "This is a pal of mine, Walter." Walter? I think I would prefer to be called Toilet Breath. Tony went on, "He's got a problem and I told him you two would help him. I hope you don't mind. Lucy's so clever at things like that."

"So am I," I said.

71

Lucy grinned. "Two heads are better than one, Tony."

Tony didn't look too sure. "Well, Walter here's been getting funny letters and we don't know who's sending them."

Walter gave Lucy a letter to look at.

The writing was bad and the spelling was really awful.

YU AR IN REEL TRUBEL. AM GONNY GET U WUN DAY SOON.

"What do you want us to do about it?" Lucy asked.

"Well, we thought you and Greg could find out who's sending them."

Lucy did one of those annoying laughs of hers. "Who do you think we are? Sherlock Holmes and Doctor Watson?"

I took the letter from Lucy. "I've found the first clue," I said. "This letter is from

72

someone who can't spell. That means it could be anybody in this school."

"Brilliant!" Lucy said in a very sarcastic voice. "What would I do without you, Doctor Watson?"

Doctor Watson, indeed. "Hey! I'm the Sherlock Holmes in this team," I told her.

But ever since then, that's what me and Lucy have been. A team.

Barrington Stoke would like to thank all its readers for commenting on the manuscript before publication and in particular:

Kirsty Baldwin	Nicola Parker
Matthew Belton	Heather Podmore
Pat Brockman	Kath Podmore
Barbara Cradock	Sam Price
Jessica English	Michelle Procter
Kirsten Knight	Diane Smale
Belinda Langrish	Jade Spillman
James Langrish	Zainab Tahir
Laura Lees	Emily Whittaker
Tyrone Palmer	

Become a Consultant!

Would you like to give us feedback on our titles before they are published? Contact us at the address below – we'd love to hear from you!

Barrington Stoke, Sandeman House, Trunk's Close,
55 High Street, Edinburgh EH1 1SR
Tel: 0131 557 2020 Fax: 0131 557 6060
Email: info@barringtonstoke.co.uk
Website: www.barringtonstoke.co.uk